Rosy Cole:

She Walks in Beauty

Rosy Cole:

She Walks in Beauty

by **Sheila Greenwald**

Little, Brown and Company
Boston New York Toronto London

First Edition

The characters and events portrayed in this book are fictitious. Any similarity to real persons, living or dead, is coincidental and not intended by the author.

Library of Congress Cataloging-in-Publication Data

Greenwald, Sheila.
    Rosy Cole : she walks in beauty / by Sheila Greenwald. — 1st ed.
        p. cm.
    Summary: Rosy finds out how difficult it is to become one of the beautiful people.
    ISBN 0-316-32743-3
    [1. Beauty, Personal—Fiction.]   I. Title.   II. Title: She walks in beauty.
PZ7.G852Rne   1994
[Fic]—dc20   93-40114

10 9 8 7 6 5 4 3 2 1

BP

Published simultaneously in Canada
by Little, Brown & Company (Canada) Limited

Printed in the United States of America

For Lila

Rosy Cole:

She Walks in Beauty

Chapter One

I was with my friend Christi McCurry, checking out the new stuff in La Dream Teen Boutique on Madison Avenue, when I overheard one saleslady say to the other, "What a beautiful child."

Even though I don't like to be called a child, I turned to smile at them.

"That hair, that skin," the saleslady gushed, "those dimples. Do you diet?"

"Never," Christi snapped.

"Oh my, she was born that way." The saleswoman wrung her hands she was so happy. "You could be a model, dear."

"I *am* a model," Christi told them. "It's very hard work."

"You are one fortunate little girl to get it. Why don't you try on this velvet? I'd love to see you in it." She snatched the dress right out of my hands, and Christi did her the favor of trying it on.

I picked out another party dress and held it under my chin.

t's a delicate fabric," the sales-
irned me, "and it isn't your size."
wed the dress to Christi. "Would
you try this one on too, dear? Perhaps
when we do our next fashion show, you'd
model for us. You are a perfect four."

"*I* am a four," I volunteered.

"A *perfect* four," the saleslady repeated.

"You'll have to call my agent." Christi
fished around in her knapsack. "Here's
his card. He arranges all my bookings. I
do preteen sizes. My sister Dawn does
junior miss. She charges less than I do."
She handed the dress back to the
saleslady and took off the velvet. "I have
no time to try on anything else now."
Christi winked at me. "My friend and I
are in a hurry."

I was happy to hear Christi call me
her friend since we certainly didn't start
out that way. When she arrived in my

class last fall, the first thing she did was form a club that specialized in hairdos, attracting boys, and calling anybody not in it a baby. It wasn't until we "babies" made our Valentine's Day party so much better than hers that she invited us all to join her club.

Out on the street I started to notice something I'd never really noticed before.

Christi walking down Madison Avenue was different from me walking down Madison Avenue.

Even Mike the doorman opening the door for Christi

was different from Mike the doorman opening the door for me.

By the time we got back to the building where we both live, I knew two things:

1. A Beautiful Person has a different life.

2. A Beautiful Person has a better life.

My name is Rosy Cole. I live on the
Upper East Side of Manhattan with my
parents, Sue and Mike, and my sisters,
Anitra and Pippa, and a cat named Pie.
We are all okay to look at, but none of us
is beautiful. I decided I was going to do
anything I could to change that.

THE COLE FAMILY

Chapter Two

The next day was Friday. Friday is half day at my school. I go to Reed, a small private school for girls near where I live. At Reed we wear uniforms so we don't get distracted by appearance, and we pay attention to important things like studying. But even in her uniform, Christi is a standout.

Usually I walk home from school with Christi and Hermione Wong, since we all live in the same building. Sometimes on Friday we stop for a slice at Vinnie's or visit each other's apartment.

"I can't go for pizza today," Christi told us. "I have a shoot this afternoon and Dawn is going to prepare my face so I'm knock-out beautiful."

Hermione and I went into Vinnie's and ordered a slice and a root beer each.

"What's the matter, Rosy?" Hermione asked. "You're not like you."

"I want to be knock-out beautiful too," I blurted. "And I don't know how."

"You look okay," Hermione told me. "My dad says you have personality. He says there's nobody like Rosy."

"I don't want personality. I want nice dimples and skin and hair and people saying I'm beautiful and acting like they do to Christi."

"Christi is a professional model," Hermione reminded me. "She couldn't even come for pizza with us. Right now, as we sit here eating slices, she's trying to make herself gorgeous."

I jumped up from the table and put on my jacket. "Right now, instead of sitting here eating slices, we should be finding out how she does it."

Hermione wrapped her leftover pizza in a napkin and put it in her knapsack. "I suppose I could pick up a few pointers," she said.

Christi's brother, Donald, opened the door to her apartment. He is in the eighth grade at Finchely, our brother school. Donald is always thinking about something so important that he never sees me. This is a shame since when I look at him, I feel all fizzy like soda water. "Where is Christi?" I asked him.

"Follow the smell of hair spray." Donald glared down the hall.

Christi was in her sister Dawn's room, sitting in front of a special model's mirror. Dawn was making her up.

"Can we watch?" I asked.

"Just pull up a chair," Dawn said. "I'll teach you the tricks of the trade."

I took out my notebook and pencil.

Dawn had loads of little bottles and tubes of color. With brushes and sponges and wads of cotton she patted the colors onto Christi's face.

"Any questions?" she asked.

"What are you doing?" Hermione said.

"I'm giving her a natural look," Dawn explained. "My beauty philosophy is to strive for what is natural."

I wrote this in my notebook.

"For a natural look you need a large palette of colors," Dawn went on.

Hermione and I both made a list of all the different colors that went into Christi's natural look.

When Christi was ready to leave for her shoot, we went back to my place to find the palette I would need.

From my sisters' and my mother's makeup drawers we could come up with only five lipsticks, three tubes of color rub, and a dried mascara.

13

"We need a bigger palette," I said.

"We need the Cosmetic Barn," Hermi-one said.

Fortunately it was only two blocks away.

Chapter Three

Halfway down aisle 3 of the Cosmetic Barn we spotted Lori.

"Can you make me over?" I asked her.

Lori looked around nervously. "I don't know if this offer extends to people your age," she said. "But since I'm a little slow right now . . . why not?" She patted the stool.

I hopped up.

Lori turned a bright light on my face and studied it.

While she studied my face, I studied hers. I didn't ask about her beauty philosophy. I was afraid it was Masks.

"What I like to do is bring out your good points and hide the bad ones," Lori said. "For example, you've got lovely big brown eyes, but your hair has no body." She began to tease my hair with a comb. "Your skin is nice, but your color is pale. What kind of look do you want?"

"Natural," I said.

"Of course."

She put a towel under my chin, sprayed my face with cold water, and

16

wiped it clean. Soon she was patting stuff on just like Dawn. She put color on my cheeks and body in my hair. She outlined my eyes and brought out my lips. "There you go, sweetheart." She whipped off the towel.

"Wow," Hermione gasped. "You look like somebody else."

"Like who?" I asked.

"Like Lori," she said.

Walking back to our building, I was getting reactions all right. But were they for my beauty? How could I tell? Then Mike the doorman burst out laughing. "Somebody hit you with a paint box, Rosy?" he asked.

I could tell.

I said good-bye to Hermione at her floor. "Nothing happens overnight," she consoled me. "Beauty included."

My sisters were in the kitchen eating pretzels.

Anitra took off her dark glasses to get a better look at me.

"Weird, baby, weird."

19

My parents walked in the door carrying groceries. Mom nearly dropped her bag.

My sister Pippa pulled up a chair for me. "Tell us about it, Rosy," she said.

"I want to be beautiful," I blubbered.

"Beautiful?" My father set down his packages. "Beauty isn't a ton of goop and powder."

"Beauty is something inside that shines through," Mom added. "Character and spirit."

"Beauty is the saleslady at Dream Teen Boutique telling you you're a perfect size four," I informed them. "Beauty is everybody smiling at you just because you smile back with dimples."

"Nobody in our family ever had dimples," Mom said.

"Nobody in our family ever had beauty either," I cried. "But I'm going to change that, if it's the only thing I ever do!"

20

I ran to the bathroom and looked in the mirror. Koko the Clown looked back.

I washed off every bit of goop.

When I came back out, my family was very quiet. Finally Mom said, "Rosy, dear, real beauty is not found in tubes and jars."

"Where, then?"

"In poetry and music and great works of art. You can be sure the Venus de Milo didn't wear pancake makeup."

"She doesn't have a head either," Pippa said.

"Who's Venus de Milo?" I asked.

"Venus was the goddess of beauty in ancient Rome," my mother told me. "Throughout time, artists and sculptors have depicted her. The Venus de Milo is a famous statue. It *does* have a head. Its arms are missing. With or without arms, you can find more real beauty in the great art museums than at any cosmetic counter."

"The great art museums?" I repeated. I couldn't believe my good luck. We live only five blocks from the Metropolitan Museum of Art.

Chapter Four

Saturday morning I made sure I was at the museum just as the doors opened. But once I was inside, I didn't know where to begin. Then I saw Venus. . . .

The problem was, I saw her over and over again.

I saw her fat and thin and fair and dark. I was about to give up when all of a sudden I saw Donald McCurry.

"What are you doing here?" I asked.
"Working on my school project." He

held up his notepad to show me. " 'Ideals of Beauty in Ancient Greek Urns.' What are you doing here?"

"It's personal."

"Personal?" Donald actually looked at me. "Are you interested in great art too?"

"I'm interested in learning the lessons it can teach."

"So am I." Donald said this as if he couldn't believe his ears. "I want to be an art historian."

"I want to be beautiful," I found myself confiding. Donald and I had never had a conversation this long. "I was told great art could help me become as beautiful as Dawn and Christi."

"Dawn and Christi? Beautiful?" Donald practically groaned.

"Strangers smile at Christi when she walks down the street," I informed him. "They love her natural style."

"She paints herself up like a billboard and calls it natural. You don't need that stuff, Rosy."

"Don't tell me I have personality," I said. "Because personality isn't enough." I pointed to a painting on the wall behind him. "That is what I want."

Donald studied the painting and shook his head. "Not your type."

"How do you know?"

"I spend a lot of time in the museum, so I've picked up a thing or two. I know more about beauty than both my sisters put together, and they never even ask my opinion."

It occurred to me that bumping into Donald might be my lucky break in more ways than one. "*I'm* asking your opinion," I said. "Maybe you could be my guide to beauty."

Donald turned his green eyes on my face. They were the color of the ocean, so cool and deep I felt as if I could swim in them.

"If I apply my beauty philosophy to your problem," he told me, "I think I can help. But first you must promise to do what I say."

"I promise."

Donald nodded solemnly. "Then follow me."

I followed him
from painting to
painting and
did whatever
I could to
help
him.

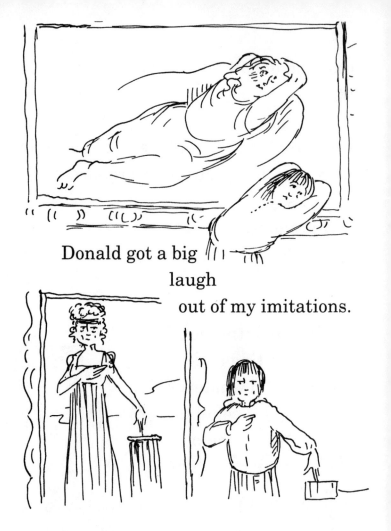

Donald got a big laugh out of my imitations.

"You are more fun to be with than any girl I ever met," he said.

"But this is no joke," I reminded him. "You must help me find my beauty type."

Suddenly he stopped in his tracks.
"There she is," he said.

"Be serious."

"Come," Donald beckoned. "I'll show
you." He *was* serious.

Down in the museum shop, Donald picked out a book of postcards. "Study these." He handed me the book. "Then copy the models in the paintings until you can hold your head, your hands, your wrists, and your neck the way they do. Work in front of the mirror. The more you practice, the better." He began to write on a page from his notebook.

"You'll need these, too." He paid for the cards and gave them to me with the list. "You can do it, Rosy Cole," Donald said. "You're on your way."

"Where am I going, Donald?" I asked.

He closed his eyes and lifted his brows. "'She walks in beauty,'" he said, "'like the night / Of cloudless climes and starry skies.'"

"That's wonderful," I whispered. "Did you just make it up?"

He shook his head. His face was red, right down to the neck. "It's a poem by Lord Byron. I love poetry."

"Me too." I nodded. From that moment on, I did love poetry. Only *I* wouldn't just walk in beauty, I'd run.

Chapter Five

Sunday morning I asked my sister Anitra if I could borrow eight dollars for a home perm kit.

"You can use mine." She led me into the bathroom and took a box out of the cabinet. "Since I'm letting my hair grow out straight, I won't need this anymore." Anitra handed me the box and I opened it.

"What do I owe you?" I asked.

"Five nights of my turn at kitchen cleanup."

"Oh no," I groaned.

"Three, then." Anitra reached for the box. "That's my final offer."

I clutched the box to me.

"Home perms are hard to do," Anitra warned.

I unfolded the instruction sheet that was inside the package. "If I follow these simple directions, it will be as easy as ABC," I said.

After she left my room, I found out
ABC can be very complicated.

When Anitra knocked on my door and offered to give me a hand, I was so grateful I promised her two extra nights of kitchen cleanup.

"I hope you'll still be grateful when the rollers come out." Anitra set the timer.

"What do you mean?" I began to worry. "I won't blame you."

"But Mom and Dad will."

I kept my eyes shut tight while Anitra unrolled my hair. Then I heard her sigh and say, "Wow. Rosy, take a look."

I took a look. "You have helped me begin my walk in beauty," I told my sister.

"Where are you headed?" Anitra asked.

I showed her the pictures Donald had given me.

Anitra nodded slowly. A few minutes later she brought me some silk flowers for my hair and a green dress. "You can keep these," she said. "The dress is like the one in the painting."

I put on the dress and called Donald. I wanted him to come right over to see me. But he was out. For the rest of the day I practiced in front of the mirror.

From the postcards I chose a smile and a pose. I held up another mirror so I could view myself from different angles.

It got dark. Pippa called me in for dinner.

In the dining room my family turned to stare at me.

"Rosy, dear," my mother said. "You look like . . ."

"A painting?" Anitra suggested.

"Yes." My father beamed.

"Like a beautiful portrait," Pippa agreed.

We sat down at the table. All through dinner, I practiced posing with my wrist, my neck, my hands, my smile.

Suddenly it was time to clear the

plates and I hadn't gotten to eat very much. I didn't mind doing Anitra's turn at kitchen cleanup. I practiced while I loaded the dishwasher.

As soon as I could, I went back to my mirror. I tried sitting gracefully and crossing my legs. Then I tried doing my homework, but it was late and I was tired.

I couldn't wait to show Donald what I had accomplished. Monday morning I spent a long time preparing my appearance. But when I got down to the lobby, Donald and Christi and Hermione had already gone off to school.

"They didn't want to be late," Mike the doorman explained. Then he opened the front door for me and bowed from the waist. "Good morning to you, lovely lady Rosy," he said.

There was no question about it, something major had happened.

When I got to school, everybody in my class commented on my new appearance.

"Can I feel it, Rosy? Oh, please." Linda Dildine was already running her fingers through my hair.

"Me too." Debbie stuck her hand in before I gave her permission.

Christi said, "Nice," and Hermione just stared.

"Wow," a few people sighed, really impressed.

Even Mrs. Oliphant, my teacher, was impressed by my hair. She was also impressed that I hadn't done my homework. I told her I would hand it in to her the next day.

All through class I practiced beauty. I tried to lean on my desk the way the woman in the painting leaned. I glanced sideways and down at my books.

At lunch I gave away half of my sandwich. I needed a smaller waist.

In the library, Ms. Medoff actually clapped her hands together when she saw me. "Has Mr. Franz had a look at you?" she cried.

Mr. Franz is our art teacher. During art class I noticed that he was busy sketching while we worked. After the bell rang, he showed me what he was doing. "I couldn't resist drawing you, Rosy," he said.

I wondered if I was walking in beauty already. My family thought so, my friends thought so, even my art teacher thought so, but I wouldn't believe it until Donald thought so.

Chapter Six

I found the poem "She Walks in Beauty" and copied it to hang in my room.

> She walks in beauty, like the night
> Of cloudless climes and starry skies;
> And all That's best of dark and bright
> Meet in her aspect and her eyes:
> Thus Mellowed To That tender light
> Which heaven To gaudy day denies.

I thought of the poem while I walked. Reciting it made me feel that my face was bright and my eyes were full of tender light.

The next morning I tried to get to the lobby on time so I could catch Donald on his way to school, but he had gone.

"He takes an early math class," Christi said. "Why do you care, anyway?"

"I want to show him my new look. He was my beauty consultant," I confessed.

"My brother Donald gave you that frizzy hair?" Christi was amazed.

I didn't tell her he also gave me a frizzy feeling right down to my toenails.

Christi narrowed her eyes and squinted at me as if I were an object on a store counter that she was considering buying. "It works," she finally decided. "It might even be a look you could sell."

Hermione stepped out of the elevator.

There was something different about her.

"Nobody in my family had a home perm kit," she complained. "I was up half the night on rollers."

"Beauty is hard work," Christi said knowingly. "It's not for everybody. Some people can't handle it at all."

"You should find your own beauty type," I added. "Try not to copy another person."

"If you think for one minute that I am trying to copy *your* looks, you can forget it," Hermione stormed.

I didn't answer her, but if I had any question about anybody trying to copy my looks, I forgot it as soon as we got to school.

Something else I forgot was my home-work.

Mrs. Oliphant took me aside after class. "What has come over you, Rosy?" she asked. "This is the second day in a row you didn't hand in your assign-ment."

I tipped my head and smiled at her, the new smile that I had been practicing.

"Pretty smiles are all very well," Mrs. Oliphant said. "New haircuts are fun, but completing your school assignments will do you more good in the long run."

Just one look at Mrs. Oliphant and you knew she didn't know one thing about beauty in the long run or even the short run. She had never walked in it. She hadn't even sat in it. I kept smiling at her. "I will do my best," I promised. But I didn't say at what.

I could hardly wait till school was out. After school I headed over to Vinnie's with Debbie and Linda and Hermione. I was hungry from skipping lunch, but I didn't order any food. I just gulped water and tried not to breathe in the smell of the pizza. It looked so good I nearly reached across the counter and grabbed a whole pie. I closed my eyes and reminded myself that if I wasn't thin, I could forget about walking in beauty.

When we were all sitting at a big table in the corner, Debbie said, "Okay, Rosy, how did you do this beauty thing?"

47

"Beauty takes practice and work," I told her.

"What kind of practice and work?" Linda leaned over the table. She held her pizza slice in one hand. Her mouth was open and her eyes were huge. She was waiting to hear something very important.

"For example, you could practice keeping your mouth closed when you aren't talking," I advised her. "An open mouth looks dumb. Also, stop pulling on your bangs and try to stand up straight." I turned to Debbie. I was on a roll. "*You* could take off ten pounds and wash your hair every day so it isn't so greasy."

They both stopped eating and glared at me.

"I don't think it's worth being pretty, if it makes you stuck-up and mean," Linda whimpered.

"Beauty is hard work," I quoted Christi. "It's not for everybody. Some people can't handle it."

Debbie took a huge bite out of her slice and chewed angrily. "I'll work on beauty some other time," she said through full cheeks. "This pizza is so good, it's the only thing I feel like handling."

I almost grabbed the leftover crust right off her plate.

When Debbie finished her second slice, we all walked down Madison Avenue to check out La Dream Teen.

While my friends were examining the jewelry in a case by the front counter, I went through the rack of party dresses.

All of a sudden I saw one that practically made me faint it was so beautiful. I stood before the long mirror and held the dress under my chin.

"What a beautiful child," one saleslady cried out to the other. "Why don't you try that on, sweetheart?" They both came up behind me.

My friends were all watching while I stepped into the dressing room with the two saleswomen on either side.

When I came out of the dressing room, Linda and Debbie and Hermione were gone.

"Your friends had to leave," the saleslady said.

It isn't easy watching somebody else walk in beauty. I knew that from experience.

"One week from Saturday we're having our spring fashion show," the saleswoman said. "We think it's fun to invite some of our local customers to model for us. Could you stand as still as a statue, in our window, wearing that dress?"

"As still as a statue in the window of La Dream Teen Boutique wearing a beautiful dress? Could I ever." It was exactly what I had been dreaming of.

"We can't pay you, but there are always important fashion people watching our windows. Who knows? Modeling for us could lead to something big." The saleswoman clapped her hands as if it already had. "If you decide to join us, bring a note of permission from one of your parents."

"I hope they say yes." The second saleslady put out her hand to shake mine. "I am Miss Nina, and my partner is Miss Tilly."

I thanked Miss Nina and Miss Tilly and took off the dress. I promised I would bring them the note as soon as I could.

I stepped out of La Dream Teen and

swung my arms at my sides. Now I knew I was beautiful. I tipped back my head and tossed my hair so it flew out like a cloud. That was why I didn't see the curb and fell down.

Three people came rushing up to help me stand and to ask if I was all right. I was all right, all right. I was beautiful.

Chapter Seven

When I got home I rushed into Anitra's room to tell her about La Dream Teen Boutique's asking me to model for them.

Can't talk to you now." Anitra waved me off. She didn't even look up from her books. "If I don't get an A on these tests, I won't get into a good arts program."

"Why do you want a good arts program?"

"So I'll be accepted into design school."

I went to find Pippa. But her head was practically buried in notes. "Talk to you later," she growled. "I'm studying for the most important biology exam of my life."

"What for?"

"What for? So I have the grades I need to get into veterinary school. That's what for!"

My sisters were hopeless. They had to work hard and suffer because they would never walk in beauty . . . like me.

Finally my mother came home from work. I told her my thrilling news.

"Dream Teen Boutique wants you to model in their window?" Mom laughed. "Sounds like fun, if it doesn't interfere with your schoolwork."

I promised her it wouldn't. She wrote me a note of permission for Miss Nina.

"You have done wonders with your looks, Rosy," Mom said.

I ran to the telephone to call Donald. I told him about La Dream Teen.

"I've got to see you," Donald said, "but I can't get away right now. Can you meet

me on Saturday, at the museum? Eleven o'clock."

"I'll be in front of my portrait." I giggled.

On Saturday morning I greeted my reflection in the mirror. "Congratulations, Rosy Cole," I said. "You really did DO it." I fixed my hair and put a silk flower in it. Then I put on the dress Anitra had given me. With another flower in my hand I set out to meet Donald.

Inside the museum I went directly to *my* painting. Soon a guided tour came into the gallery. The tour guide spotted me, and her mouth fell open. "If I didn't see this with my own eyes, I wouldn't believe it. Look!" She pointed me out to her group as if I were one of the pictures

on the wall. "It's as if the painting had come to life."

They all swarmed around me. "Her hair, even her smile. It's the portrait," they said.

"What is your name, child?" the guide asked.

I was about to tell when Donald called out, "Hey, Rosy Cole."

"Rosy Cole?" The guide laughed. "You look like a Constanza or Gabriella. You could be the work of an old master of the Pre-Raphaelite school."

"She's the work of an eighth-grader at the Finchely School," Donald said proudly. "Me."

The guided tour laughed as if it were a joke. I wished Donald had kept his mouth shut. I was not in the mood to be a joke.

"You look great, Rosy," Donald said. "Come on, there's something I have to show you." He took me by the hand and pulled me through three galleries till he found what he was looking for. Donald pointed at the picture. "Can you imitate that?"

"I did not come here to do imitations," I informed him. "I am not a stand-up comic."

"I'm sorry," Donald said. "I thought you had as much fun doing them as I had watching you."

"Let's get some sodas," I suggested.

In the museum cafeteria we picked up a couple of seltzers and sat at a table facing a big window. Donald took out his sketchbook. "I wish you would take a look at these. I think they're the best I ever did." He handed me the book.

While I turned the pages of Donald's sketch pad, I admired my reflection in the window. "Very nice," I said.

"You can't take your eyes off yourself," Donald complained. He leaned across the table and took the book back. "I don't think you're interested in my drawings."

All the way home from the museum we didn't say a word. When Mike the doorman opened the door for me he bowed. "'Tis the lovely lady Rosy," he said. "What happened to the little girl I used to know?"

"She's gone." Donald sighed.

"And good riddance," I added. "Nobody ever asked her to model in a fashion show. She was not walking in beauty like the night of cloudless climes."

"But she was fun to be with. She was my friend." Donald shook his head and got out of the elevator at his floor.

What was going on here? Donald McCurry couldn't handle my beauty either?

Chapter Eight

The next morning, the minute I opened my eyes and looked in the mirror, I saw I had slept on my hair in a way that made it stick out on one side. There was a red blotch on my chin.

After breakfast I sat down to do my back math homework, but I had to keep checking to see if my hair had calmed down and if the blotch was paler. Soon all the numbers on the page began to look like pimples and stray hairs.

I couldn't concentrate.

I tried to do my history assignment. "If I Lived in Salem at the Time of the Puritans."

I read about the women who were accused of witchcraft in Salem, and what a hard time they had. I was sure if they had been pretty, everybody would have liked them better and they wouldn't have gotten into trouble. I wrote my report: "If I lived in Salem, I would have been all right, because I would have made myself so beautiful that everybody would love me."

I couldn't stretch my idea to a full page so I redid my hair and practiced in front of the mirror on and off for the rest of the day.

Monday morning my blotch was worse and my hair was still sticking out on one side. I didn't want to go to school. I put a scarf over my hair and a Band-Aid over the blotch.

When school let out, I didn't wait for my friends. I ran all the way home. I washed my hair and set it on the small rollers and tried to do my homework. Miss Nina from Dream Teen called. She asked me to stop by at the shop with my mother's note of permission. I covered my head with a scarf and rolled my turtleneck sweater up to my nose. I put on a pair of Anitra's super-dark glasses. If Miss Nina saw my hair and my skin she might change her mind about me modeling.

I put the note in my pocket and ran all the way to the shop. "Delivery from

R. Cole," I said, before anybody could ask what I wanted. I dropped the permission letter on the counter and beat it.

Wednesday and Thursday the blotch on my chin got paler, but three little red spots came out between my eyebrows. By Friday my hair was better, but the three spots were bigger. Friday afternoon my mother got a call from Mrs. Oliphant.

"Mrs. Oliphant says you are more interested in your hair and your complexion than in homework and classwork," my mother said. "Tomorrow you are going to stay home and catch up on your work."

"But I'm supposed to model for the Dream Teen Boutique spring fashion show," I reminded her.

My mother shook her head. "Modeling clothes won't help you in school."

"Beautiful people don't need school," I

67

informed her. "They can make a ton of money without opening a single book. They get invited to the best parties. Everybody wants to be with them. Everybody wants to see them."

"What happens to them later, when they aren't beautiful anymore?"

"By then they are so old, you can't imagine it." From the look on my mother's face I could tell she could imagine it. In fact I guessed *she* was probably that old. I felt sorry for her. "When people are that old they can do other things." I tried to comfort Mom. "Like design houses or go to veterinary school."

"Not if they stopped doing their schoolwork. Not if they spent all their time looking in mirrors. You are not going to be doing any modeling tomorrow." My mother left the room.

What could I do? I tried to calm myself. I tried to stay beautiful. For help I turned to the book of postcard paintings Donald had given me. I found the picture of a woman lying in a stream and holding a bunch of red flowers. She looked so lovely and so sad. Her name

was Ophelia. I filled the tub with a few inches of water and lay down in it, holding my flowers just like Ophelia.

A little while later Pippa banged on the door. "What are you doing in

there, Rosy?" She opened the door and

screamed. My mother rushed in. I sat
up.

"All right." Mom sighed. If it's that
important to you, go stand in the window of La Dream Teen Boutique. I give
up."

Of course she gave up. Beauty always
wins.

Chapter Nine

In the morning, I took a long bath with Mom's bubbles.

For breakfast I had three glasses of water and a diet cracker. Then Anitra and Pippa walked me over to La Dream Teen.

Miss Nina and Miss Tilly were waiting for me. So were the other two models. They were Vanida and Christi's sister Dawn.

First Miss Tilly did our hair.

Then Miss Nina did our faces. She squinted at Dawn's forehead. "You've got little wrinkles all over your brow," she said.

"Oh no," Dawn wailed.

"It's because you use your face too much. Try not to make expressions," Miss Tilly advised.

We put on our clothes, and Miss Nina arranged each of us in a separate frame in the window. "Perfect." Miss Tilly clapped her hands. "Now try to hold those poses no matter what." She raised the blind over the window. "You're on," she announced.

People walking down Madison Avenue stopped to look at us. A small crowd gathered. Some of them waved and smiled. I stood still. The big clock across the street said eleven o'clock.

Customers began to fill the store. I could hear them telling Miss Nina and Miss Tilly we were darling. They said my dress was a dream.

Miss Nina called, "This is our best show yet."

My arm went to sleep. It was only eleven-fifteen.

Linda Dildine came up to the window. She was with her parents. "I'm going to the zoo," she mouthed.

I didn't move or break my pose. My other arm went to sleep. My stomach growled. It said, "Feed me."

Dawn began to make funny noises.

"What's the matter with you?" Vanida asked under her breath.

"I'm starting to wrinkle and my hips are too big."

"Get a lip job," Vanida said.

"Hip, not lip. I *had* a lip job and I didn't like the way they turned out."

My right foot fell asleep. It was eleven forty-five.

Anitra and Pippa came up to the window and waved to me.

"Who are those slobs?" Vanida asked.

"Rosy's sisters don't care what they look like," Dawn said.

"They've been studying for final exams." I defended them. "They don't have time for lips and hips and wrinkles."

"Lucky them," Vanida sighed.

Debbie and Hermione waved to me. "We're going to the street fair on Park," Hermione hollered right through the window.

I love street fairs. I love the food. I could practically smell the souvlaki and hot dogs and tacos. I nearly tipped over. My left leg fell asleep.

"Everybody adores that dress," Miss Nina hissed at me. "I've had seven orders for it."

"Oh, lucky you." Dawn began to sniffle again.

"Stop that, dear," Miss Tilly told her. "It isn't pretty."

A man and a woman came into the shop. I heard them talking with Miss Nina. They were talking about me. They said they were models' agents and they were interested in booking me for other jobs. They wanted to know my name.

Dawn began to choke. "I remember when they asked for my name," she blubbered.

My arms and legs were completely numb. My face felt like plastic. All my friends were having fun while I sat in a window. If I sat long enough, I'd need a hip job or a lip job and one day I could look forward to being like Dawn... washed up.

All of a sudden I saw Donald. I wanted to scream through the window, "Help...get me out of here!" But instead I kept my pose. My heart banged so hard I was worried Miss Nina would tell me to make it stop. Donald stared at me and rolled his eyes and shook his head. I rolled my eyes and shook my head back at him.

People on the street laughed. Donald laughed. So I did it again.

Miss Tilly rushed outside to see why everybody was laughing.

"Don't make those faces," she scolded me. "Remember, you're here to look beautiful."

Donald shrugged, a great big shrug, as if to say, So now what?

I shrugged right back.

Then I reached over to the counter for Miss Nina's Magic Marker and I changed the title of my picture.

Since I had broken my pose, I climbed out of the window and took off the beautiful dress and put on my own clothes.

Donald was waiting for me on the sidewalk. "I'm heading over to the museum," he said. "Want to come?"

"Yes," I said. We crossed the street and started toward the museum. "I'll let somebody else walk in beauty," I told Donald. "It's pretty much a dead-end street. I'd rather be going someplace interesting . . . with a friend."